Mog and Mim

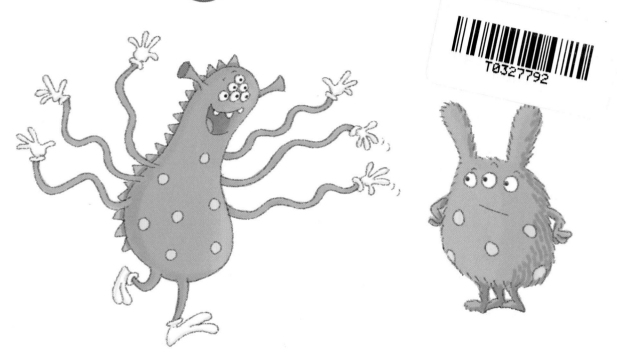

Written by Catherine Coe
Illustrated by Judy Brown

Collins

Mog and Mim hop.

Mog hops to the top.

Mim is on top.

4

Mog hops up and off.

Get fit. It is fun!

Mog huffs and puffs.

Get fit. It is fun!

Mim huffs and puffs.

Mim is in the muck!

Mog runs back up.

Mog tugs and Mim hugs.

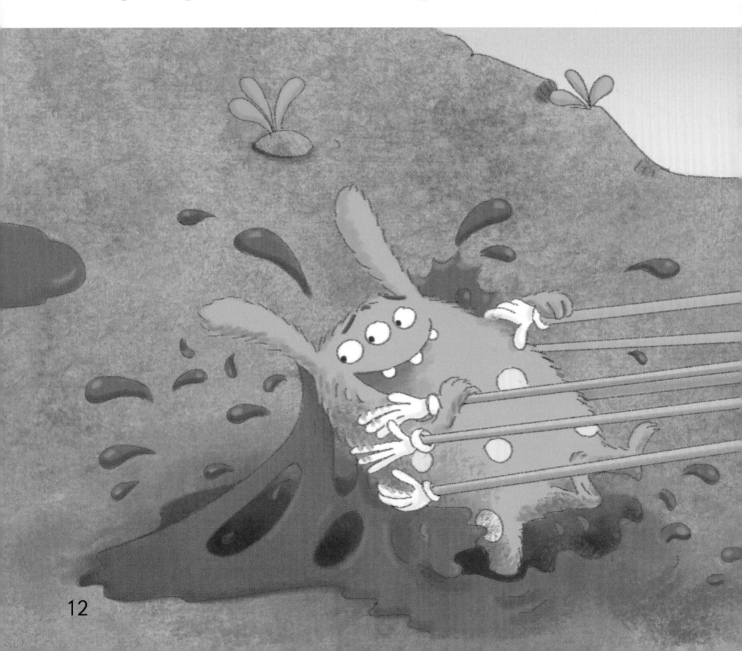

Mog picks Mim back up!

14

/f/

ff

☙ After reading ☙

Letters and Sounds: Phase 2

Word count: 55

Focus phonemes: /g/ /o/ ck /e/ /u/ /r/ /h/ /b/ /f/ ff

Common exception words: is, to, the

Curriculum links: Understanding the World: People and Communities

Early learning goals: Listening and attention: listen to stories, accurately anticipating key events and respond to what is heard with relevant comments, questions or actions; Understanding: answer 'how' and 'why' questions about experiences and in response to stories or events; Reading: children use phonic knowledge to decode regular words and read them aloud accurately; they also read some common irregular words.

Developing fluency

- Go back and read the chant to your child, using lots of expression.
- Make sure that your child follows as you read.
- Pause so they can join in and read with you.
- Say the whole chant together. You can make up some actions to go with the words.

Mog and Mim hop.	Get fit. It is fun!	Mim is in the muck!
Mog hops to the top.	Mog huffs and puffs.	Mog runs back up.
Mim is on top.	Get fit. It is fun!	Mog tugs and Mim hugs.
Mog hops up and off.	Mim huffs and puffs.	Mog picks Mim back up!

Phonic practice

- Read page 3 together. Ask your child to find two words that rhyme. (*hop, top*). Say the middle sound of each word together. Can they think of any other words that rhyme with **hop** and **top**? (e.g. *pop, mop*)
- Now do the same with page 7. (*huffs, puffs*)
- Look at the I spy sounds pages (14–15) together. Which words can your child find in the picture with the /b/, /f/ or ff sounds in them? (e.g. *puff, puffin, four, five, fizz, fox, fruit, bowl, basket, book, box*)